P9-CWD-655

For Michael,
who gave me the title
and who is always on time
—A. A.

For the Kellaway sisters—Michelle, Sara, and Natasha
—S.M-N.

Pigs on a Blanket

story by **Amy Axelrod**

pictures by **Sharon McGinley-Nally**

Simon & Schuster Books for Young Readers

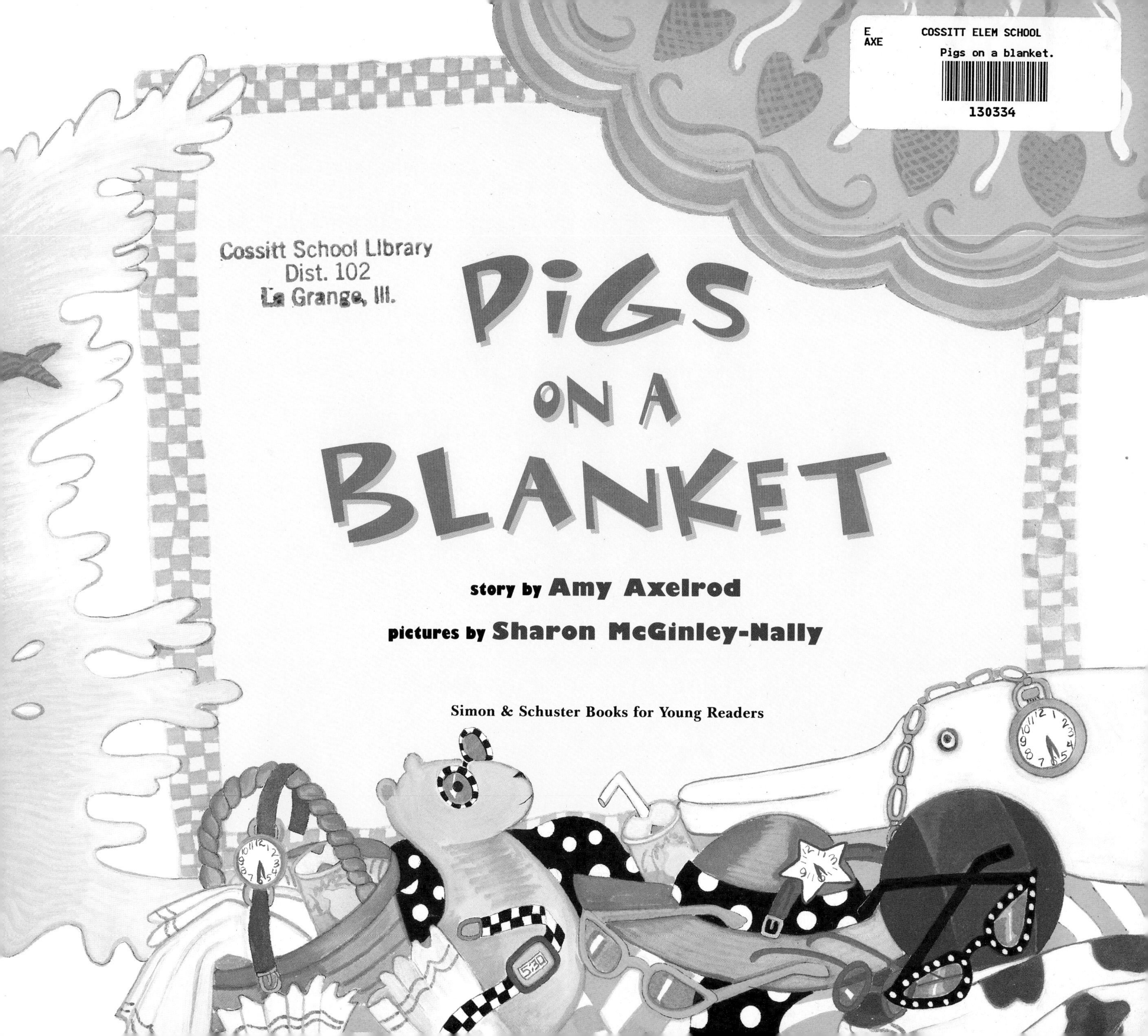

The Pigs were in a rut.

"We need a change of pace," said Mrs. Pig. "We've been glued to this couch for hours."

"Let's spend the day at the beach," suggested Mr. Pig.

"Great idea," said Mrs. Pig, "except for one thing."

"What's that?" asked Mr. Pig.

"The beach is an hour's drive from here," she said. "Don't you think we'd be getting a late start?"

Mr. Pig looked at his watch. It was 11:30. "No problem," he said. "We can be on the road in no time."

"Well then, family," said Mrs. Pig.

READY, SET, GO!

In just ten minutes, the piglets changed into swimsuits, packed beach toys, and blew up their floats.

Five minutes later, Mrs. Pig came downstairs wearing a new swimsuit and toting a bag filled with towels, hats, a blanket, sun lotion, and her favorite book.

They waited . . . and waited . . . and waited for Mr. Pig.

"It's about time!" scolded Mrs. Pig. "We've been sitting here for a good forty-five minutes. At this rate, we'll never ride the waves."

"Sorry, dear," said Mr. Pig. "I had a tough time finding a swimsuit that fit. I guess I've put on a few pounds since last year."

"Never mind," said Mrs. Pig. "Let's hurry now."

At 12:45, the Pigs were in the car and all set to leave for the beach when Mr. Pig discovered that he didn't have the car keys.

"They must be here somewhere," said Mrs. Pig.

"What do you know!" said Mr. Pig one hour later as he bent over to look under the car. "The keys were in my pocket all along."

THE ENCHANTED ENCHILADA
SLOW
FANCY FRUITS
HANK
JUST MARRIED
34X
SLOW

Finally the Pigs were on the road.
Mr. Pig made good time for
three quarters of an hour.

But then he reached a railroad crossing. Twenty-five minutes later the caboose passed, and the Pigs were once again on their way.

"Almost at the beach," said Mrs. Pig. "I can smell it in the air."

RAIL ROAD
CROSSING
BEP

"We need a bathroom," said the piglets. "It's an emergency."

"But we just passed a rest area right before the train crossing," said Mr. Pig. "Can't you wait? We'll be at the beach in just ten minutes. There's a bathroom there."

The piglets shook their heads no. "Hurry," they said.

Mr. Pig beat the clock. He made a U-turn and reached the rest area in only two minutes. While the piglets visited the bathrooms, Mr. Pig visited with a police officer who wrote him a speeding ticket. Thirteen minutes later, the police officer sent the Pigs on their way.

At 3:30, the Pigs arrived at the beach.
"We're hungry," said the piglets.

WELCOME
SHIFTING SANDS BEACH
BEACH CLOSES
5:30 P.M.
BEACH
CLOSES
5:30

Mrs. Pig and the piglets made themselves comfortable on the blanket while Mr. Pig went to the snack bar.

"I wonder what is keeping your father," said Mrs. Pig to the piglets. "He's been gone a long time."

BEACH
CLOSES
5:30

KINGS
K
K
BEACH — CLOSES
5:30
SODA
CHEESE
AVOCADO
PEANUT
OLIVE AND
ICE

A total of sixty minutes passed before Mr. Pig returned.

"The line was very long," he explained, "but it was worth the wait. Look what I brought for us to eat . . . triple-decker cheese sandwiches, chips, lemonade, and brownies."

The Pigs ate their food in ten minutes.

"We're roasting," said the piglets. "Can we go swimming now?"

"In due time," said Mrs. Pig. "Let's see, we each had a triple-decker cheese sandwich. That alone is a twenty-minute wait. Then figure ten more minutes for the chips."

"Dear, don't forget the lemonade and those delicious brownies," said Mr. Pig.

Mrs. Pig thought for a second. "Mmmm, you're right. I'm adding on an extra twenty minutes," she said, "just to be on the safe side."

The Pigs decided to pass the time relaxing on the blanket.

4:40

When their stomachs settled, Mrs. Pig said, "Okay, family, it's time to ride the waves!"

Mr. Pig led the charge to the water. "Your mother's right, kids," he said. "It's time to ride the . . ."

How Did the Pigs Run Out of Time?

It was eleven-thirty when the decided to go the . The were ready in ten minutes. was ready in fifteen minutes. But took one hour to get ready. The were in the by but could not find the . He found the after the looked for one hour. The drove for forty-five minutes until they reached the and stopped. Twenty-five minutes later the passed and the drove on. At the needed a , so made a U-turn and reached the in two minutes. visited with the for thirteen minutes. Finally at three-thirty the arrived at the . went to the , got stuck in a big ______ , and returned at with . The ate in ten minutes and insisted that the digest their for twenty minutes plus ten more minutes for the , plus an extra twenty minutes for the and , just to be on the safe side. So the relaxed on the until five-thirty when they were ready to ride the . Too bad for the !
The closes at five-thirty today and the are out of time!

Simon & Schuster Books for Young Readers
An imprint of Simon & Schuster Children's Publishing Division
1230 Avenue of the Americas, New York, NY 10020

Designed by Anahid Hamparian
The text of this book is set in 17-point Baskerville. The illustrations are rendered in inks, watercolors, and acrylics.
Manufactured in the United States of America First Edition 10 9 8 7 6 5 4 3 2
Library of Congress Cataloging-in-Publication Data.
Axelrod, Amy. Pigs on a blanket / by Amy Axelrod; pictures by Sharon McGinley-Nally.
p. cm. Summary: Because the Pig family has so many delays in getting to the beach, when they finally are ready to swim they find that the beach is closed.
ISBN 0-689-80505-5 [1. Pigs—Fiction. 2. Beaches—Fiction. 3. Time—Fiction.] I. McGinley-Nally, Sharon, ill. II. Title.
PZ7.A96155Ph 1996 [E]—dc20 95-3677

Time Facts

60 seconds = 1 minute
60 minutes = 1 hour
24 hours = 1 day

The long hand of a clock is called the minute hand. It goes around the clock once every hour. The short hand of a clock is called the hour hand. It goes around the clock twice every day, once for the A.M. hours (between midnight and noon) and once for the P.M. hours (between noon and midnight).

Some clocks have a very small hand, called the second hand. It goes around the clock once every minute. Some clocks do not have a face or hands. They are called digital clocks. The numbers, or digits, on the clock are displayed just as they would be written. For example:

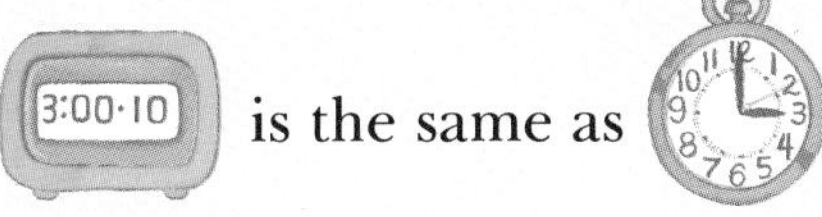

How long does it actually take the Pigs to drive to the beach?
How much longer is the drive than it should have been?
Bonus question: *How long does Mrs. Pig decide that the Pigs have to wait before they can ride the waves?*